DEATH THE DINOSAUR

NICOLAS BRASCH

NELSON
CENGAGE Learning

Australia • Brazil • Japan • Korea • Mexico • Singapore • Spain • United Kingdom • United States

Death of the Dinosaur

Fast Forward
Green Level 13

Text: Nicolas Brasch
Editor: Kate McGough
Design: James Lowe
Illustrations: Luke Jurevisius
Series design: James Lowe
Production Controller: Emma Hayes
Photo Research: Gillian Cardinal
Audio Recordings: Juliet Hill, Picture Start
Spoken by: Matthew King & Abbe Holmes
Reprint: Siew Han Ong

Acknowledgements
The author and publisher would like to acknowledge
permission to reproduce material from the following sources:
Photographs by Australian Picture Library/Corbis/Jonathan
Blair, p4 left; Natural History Museum, p5; photolibrary.
com/SPL, pp4 right, 8 top & bottom, 19, 22/Oxford Scientific
Films, p18.

ISBN 978 0 17 012583 3
ISBN 978 0 17 012573 4 (set)

Cengage Learning Australia
Level 7, 80 Dorcas Street
South Melbourne, Victoria Australia 3205
Phone: 1300 790 853

Cengage Learning New Zealand
Unit 4B Rosedale Office Park
331 Rosedale Road, Albany, North Shore NZ 0632
Phone: 0800 449 725

For learning solutions, visit **cengage.com.au**

Printed in China by 1010 Printing International Ltd
9 10 11 12 13 14 19 18 17 16 15

Evaluated in independent research by staff from the
Department of Language, Literacy and Arts Education
at the University of Melbourne.

DEATH OF THE DINOSAUR

NICOLAS BRASCH

Contents

Chapter 1

DINOSAURS ON EARTH

People know a lot about **dinosaurs**,
but they still have different ideas about how they died.

scientists studying dinosaur fossils

Triassic

Jurassic

Dinosaurs lived on Earth during a time called the Mesozoic Era.
This was between 245 million years ago and 65 million years ago.
This means dinosaurs lived on Earth for about 180 million years.

The Mesozoic Era has three parts:
the Triassic, the Jurassic and the Cretaceous.

Different dinosaurs lived at different times, within these three parts.

Cretaceous

At the start of the Mesozoic Era,
the land on Earth
was all joined together.

During the Mesozoic Era,
the land started to split apart.
This splitting apart of the land
formed the **continents**
that are on Earth today.

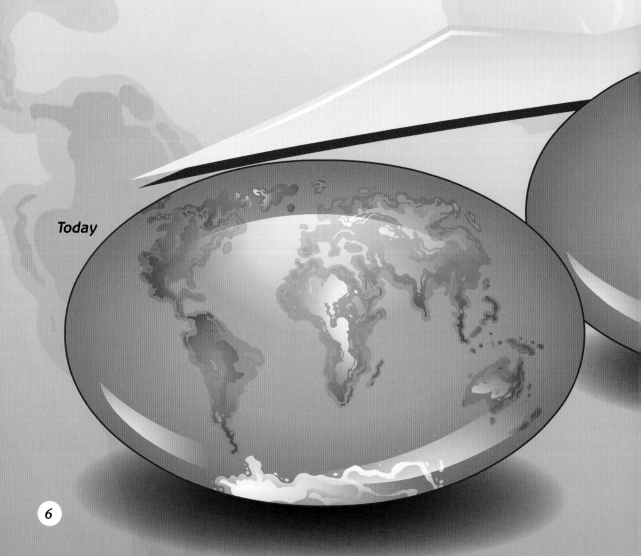

Today

245 million years ago

190 million years ago

135 million years ago

65 million years ago

Chapter 2

65 MILLION YEARS AGO

Scientists know that all the dinosaurs on Earth died out about 65 million years ago.

Scientists know this because they have studied dinosaur **fossils**.

They have also studied the earth that the fossils were found in.

Not all scientists agree about what made the dinosaurs die out.

Some scientists believe that dinosaurs died out after a **meteorite** hit the Earth.

Other scientists believe that dinosaurs died out
after the Earth's **climate** changed suddenly
because of **natural** events.

Chapter 3

A HUGE METEORITE

There are two main reasons why some scientists believe that the dinosaurs died out soon after a meteorite hit the Earth.

First, the fossils they have studied show that all of the dinosaurs died at about the same time.

If a meteorite hit the Earth,
a lot of dust would have blocked out the sun.
Without light and heat from the sun,
the dinosaurs would have died very quickly.

Second, scientists believe
that the dinosaurs died out because of a meteorite
as they have found a metal called **iridium** in rock fossils.

Iridium is a very hard metal, found in many meteorites.

Scientists have found iridium in rock fossils
near where they have found dinosaur fossils.

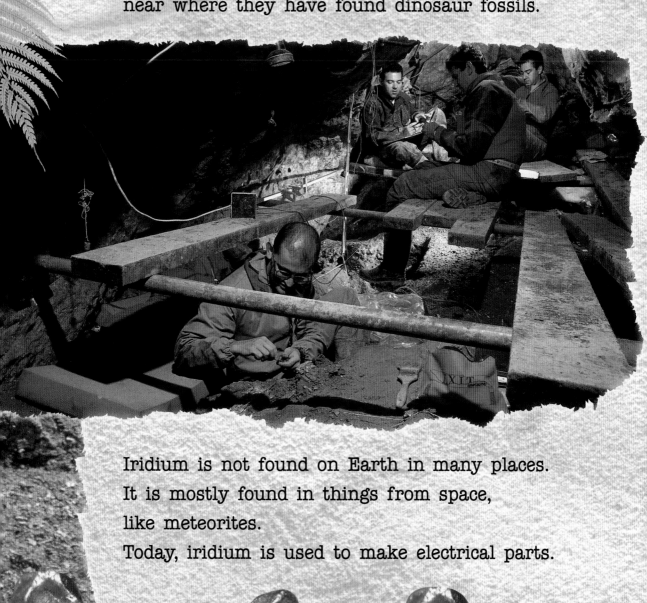

Iridium is not found on Earth in many places.
It is mostly found in things from space,
like meteorites.
Today, iridium is used to make electrical parts.

iridium

Scientists have found a **crater** that they believe was made after a meteorite hit the Earth, around 65 million years ago.

This crater is near the coastline of Mexico.

Mexico

Gulf of Mexico

Chicxulub Crater

Many scientists now believe it was this meteorite that made the dinosaurs die out.

Chapter 4

A CHANGING EARTH

Some scientists believe that natural events on Earth led to the dinosaurs dying out.

These scientists believe that volcanoes **erupted** when big parts of the land moved.
This would have changed Earth's climate.

As the climate on Earth changed, plants died.
Without plants to eat,
the plant-eating dinosaurs
would have died.
When the plant-eating dinosaurs died out,
the meat-eating dinosaurs would not have had food to eat.
They also would have died out.

Chapter 5

CONCLUSION

The Meteorite Believers say that:

- Dinosaurs died at about the same time.
- It is likely that the metal iridium,
  found in rocks near fossils,
  came from something in space.
- A crater near Mexico may have been made by
  a meteorite at around the time the dinosaurs died out.

The Changing Earth Believers say that:

- Dinosaurs died out slowly.
- There was a lot of movement on Earth
  65 million years ago.
- The movement on Earth would have changed
  Earth's climate.
  Dinosaurs would have died when the climate changed.

Glossary

climate the usual weather conditions of an area

continents Earth's seven main land masses

crater a large hole in the Earth's surface, sometimes found underwater

dinosaurs reptiles that lived during the Mesozoic era

erupted ejected lava

fossils the remains or tracks of a plant or animal, hardened in rock

iridium a hard metal, found in many meteorites

meteorite a part of a meteor that reaches the Earth's surface without burning up

natural part of nature

Index

Travelling Around

Nicolas Brasch

NELSON
CENGAGE Learning

Australia • Brazil • Japan • Korea • Mexico • Singapore • Spain • United Kingdom • United States

NELSON
CENGAGE Learning™

Travelling Around

Fast Forward
Blue Level 10

Text: Nicolas Brasch
Editor: Johanna Rohan
Design: James Lowe
Series design: James Lowe
Production controller: Hanako Smith
Photo research: Michelle Cottrill
Audio recordings: Juliet Hill, Picture Start
Spoken by: Matthew King and Abbe Holmes
Reprint: Jennifer Foo

Acknowledgements
The author and publisher would like to acknowledge
permission to reproduce material from the following sources:
Photographs by Fairfax Photos/ Peter Rae, p 9/ Wade Laube,
pp 8 top, 14 bottom; Getty Images/ Image Bank, p 4 bottom/
Stone, p 12/ Taxi, pp 5 top, 13 top; Istockphoto.com, pp 3, 6, 14
top; Newsphotos/ Lawrence Pinder, p 10 bottom/ Stuart
McEvoy, p 10 top/ Tom Campbell, p 11; Photolibrary.com/ AGE
Fotostock/ Ken Welsh, p 7/ Dynamic Graphics, pp 13 bottom,
15 bottom/ Imagestate, p 8 bottom/ Superstock, p 4 top;
Photos.com, pp 5 bottom, 15 top.

ISBN 978 0 17 012544 4
ISBN 978 0 17 012537 6 (set)

Cengage Learning Australia
Level 7, 80 Dorcas Street
South Melbourne, Victoria Australia 3205
Phone: 1300 790 853

Cengage Learning New Zealand
Unit 4B Rosedale Office Park
331 Rosedale Road, Albany, North Shore NZ 0632
Phone: 0508 635 766

For learning solutions, visit cengage.com.au

Printed in Australia by Ligare Pty Ltd
7 8 9 10 11 12 13 21 20 19 18 17

THE UNIVERSITY OF
MELBOURNE

Evaluated in independent research by staff from the
Department of Language, Literacy and Arts Education
at the University of Melbourne.

Travelling Around

Nicolas Brasch

Contents

Chapter 1

INTRODUCTION

People use lots of different ways
to travel from one place
to another place.
Some people travel on a bus.
Many people travel by car.

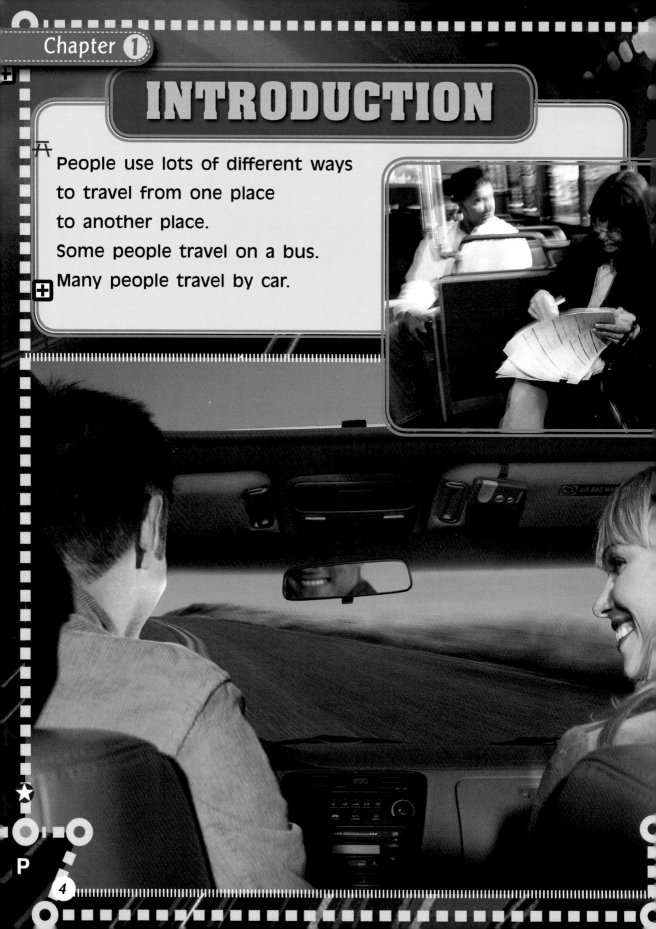

Some people walk.
Other people ride bikes.

There are good points
and bad points about all these
kinds of transport.

Chapter 2

TRAVELLING BY CAR

Cars are good for travelling long distances. They are comfortable and get people to where they are going very quickly.

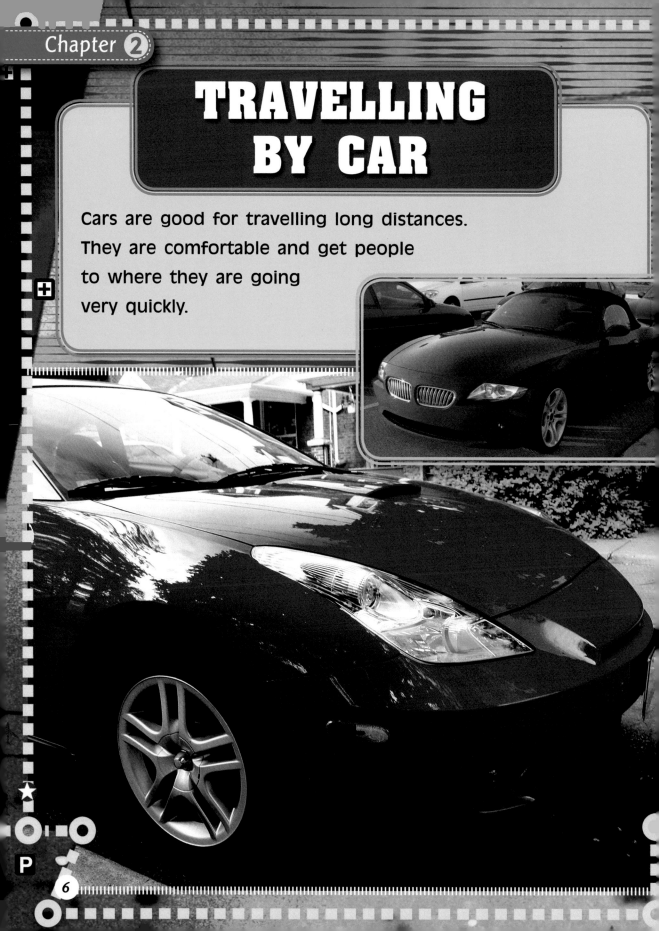

However, cars use **petrol** and
this is bad for the **environment**.
When petrol is burnt, it makes harmful gases,
which can make people sick.

TRAVELLING BY BUS

Buses are good for carrying a lot of people at one time.
It costs less money to travel on a bus
than it costs to run a car.

Running Words 117

However, some buses use a kind of petrol
that is bad for the environment.
This can make people sick.
Also, people have to wait for a bus
and can't always go to places when they want to.

TRAVELLING BY BIKE

Bikes don't cost a lot of money to run, and they don't harm the environment. Also, riding a bike is very good exercise. Bikes are good for people who can't drive a car.

However, bikes aren't as fast as cars or buses.
It can also be hard to find a safe place to park a bike
when it has to be left outside.

TRAVELLING ON FOOT

Walking is very good exercise, like riding a bike.
It doesn't cost anything to walk.

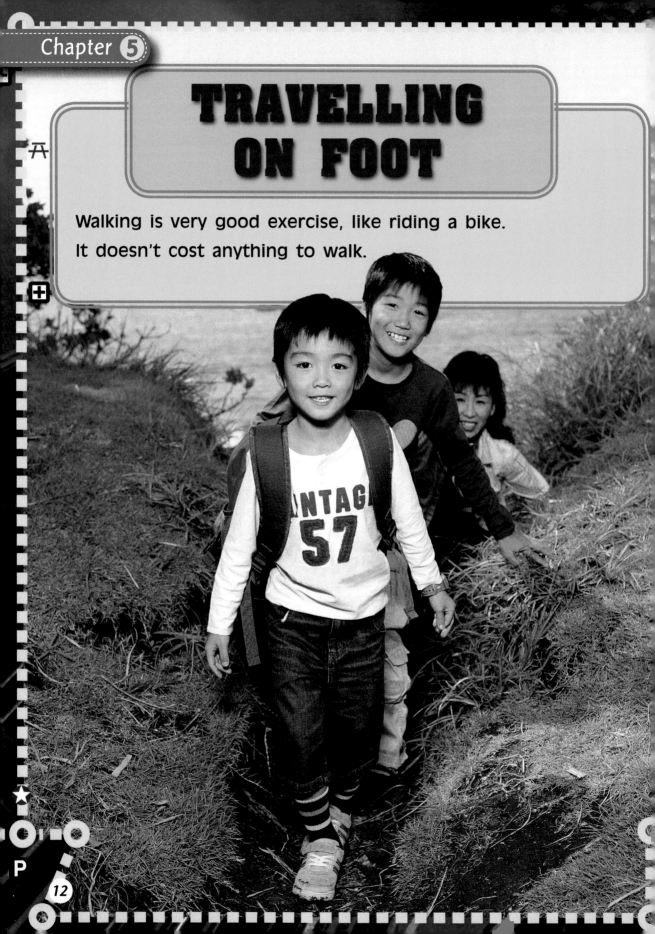

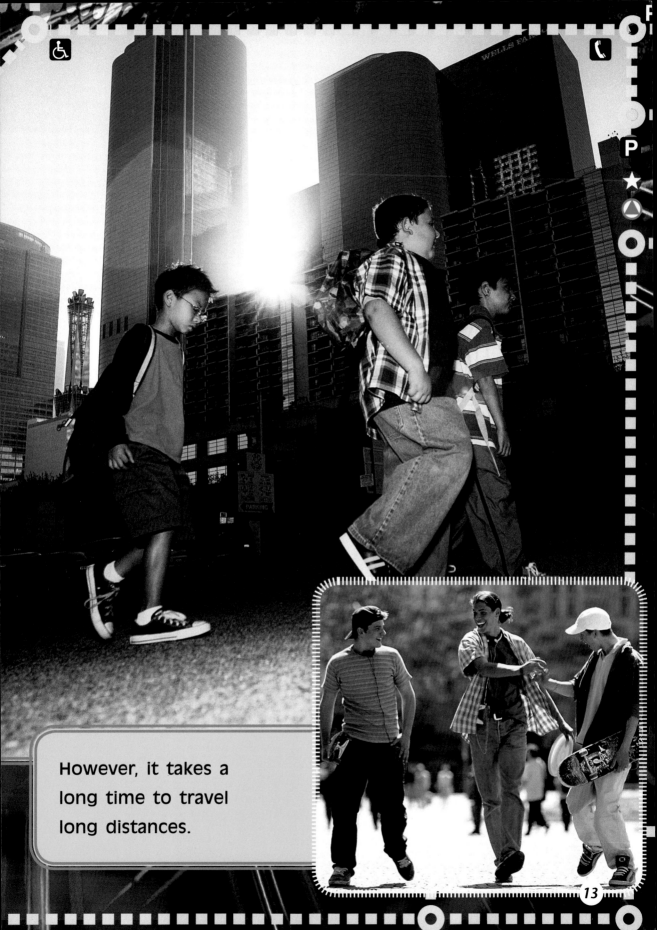

However, it takes a long time to travel long distances.

Chapter 6

PROS AND CONS

Travelling by Car

Pros

- Good for travelling long distances
- Comfortable
- Gets people around quickly

Cons

- Bad for the environment
- Burnt petrol can make people sick

Travelling by Bus

Pros

- Can carry a lot of people at one time
- Costs less than running a car

Cons

- Bad for the environment
- Have to wait for a bus to come

Travelling by Bike

Pros

- Doesn't harm the environment
- Good exercise
- Good for people who can't drive

Cons

- Not as fast as cars or buses
- Hard to find a safe place to keep outside

Travelling on Foot

Pros

- Good exercise
- Doesn't cost anything

Cons

- Takes a long time to travel a long distance
- Hard to get to places quickly

Glossary

environment   the world around us

petrol   a type of fuel used in motor vehicles

Index